WHEN LIGHT TAKES HOLD

A PREQUEL TO THE CASCADIA MYSTERIES

AVERY WILDE

This is a work of fiction. Any resemblance to actual persons or events is coincidental.

Library of Congress Control Number: 2026909540
Hardcover ISBN: 979-8-9999762-1-5
Paperback ISBN: 979-8-9999762-0-8
Ebook ISBN: 979-8-9999762-2-2

1

WHAT SHOULD THIS FEEL LIKE

The rendering had been sitting on his screen for six days.

Cole had looked at it that morning the way he'd been looking at it all week — checking the proportions, running the sight lines, measuring what was there against what could have been — and what he felt was nothing. Which was, he'd understood that morning, its own kind of answer.

The tower was eighteen stories of glass and reclaimed steel on a corner lot in Belltown that deserved better than what it was becoming. Early in the design phase, before the investor committee had weighed in, there had been something worth protecting in the proportions — a setback on the upper floors that would have let the building breathe, and a ground-level entrance that would have invited people in rather than processing them. He'd argued for both in two separate meetings. Lost both times.

What remained was clean, inoffensive, and designed primarily to photograph well in a brochure. The committee had used the word "branding" eleven times in the last meeting. Cole had counted.

He had known for a while — longer than he'd admitted — that this was the shape of things now. Too many projects are shaped by investor committees rather than intention. Deadlines that left no room for curiosity or resonance, or for the question that had mattered to him since school: what should this feel like? That question had no oxygen at the firm. And quietly, privately, Cole had come to understand that the work was starting to erase parts of himself — the parts that had wanted to build something worth building in the first place.

He saved the file, closed the laptop, and sat with his hands flat on the desk.

The office moved quietly around him. Across the room, a framed AIA Honor Award caught the afternoon light — the Salish Sea Orca Center, San Juan Island, four years earlier. A small public education center for a marine research organization, perched on pilings at the water's edge in Friday Harbor. Cole had made the ferry crossing from Anacortes more times than he could count during that project — the hour-and-a-half passage through the archipelago, islands appearing and disappearing in the mist, the water changing color as the channel deepened. He'd learned things about tidal forces on that job he hadn't learned in school.

The building sat partly over open water, and without the right engineering, the tide would have transmitted its rhythm directly through the pilings into the structure — a low, constant shudder, imperceptible to most people but present, the sea insisting on being felt. Cole had designed an isolation system that absorbed both the tidal shudder and the low-frequency mechanical noise of human occupation.

The orcas whose territory ran through those straits communicated in frequencies that could travel for miles. A building in their path needed to be acoustically invisible to them, or it wasn't a research center — it was an intrusion. The building breathed with the tide rather than fighting it, and the water beneath it remained undisturbed.

The lowest level faced the water through a full glass wall — not a window, a wall — so visitors stood as if at the boundary of two worlds, the tidal life moving past on the other side. Research vessels docked directly beneath the building overhang, out of the weather, gear unloaded without ever leaving the structure's shelter. Cole had never been more certain of anything he'd built.

The frame needed dusting. He'd stopped noticing it years ago.

Wren, his assistant, appeared in the doorway. "The Nakamura site visit is on your calendar for Thursday."

"Move it to Marcus," Cole said. "He's ready for it."

She nodded once — no pause, no question this time. Over the last several weeks, she'd fielded the client transfer letters, rescheduled the consultants, and quietly ensured Marcus had everything he needed for each handoff. The Nakamura project was the last one still on Cole's desk. "I'll let him know," she said, and pulled the door closed.

Cole sat a moment longer, then opened his email and typed a short note to the managing partner. He read it once, made no changes, and sent it.

David Marsh appeared in his doorway twenty minutes later. He was a tall man who had built the firm from twelve people to sixty and who had, in Cole's experience, never once raised his voice. He stood with his hands in his pockets and looked at Cole the way he looked at a building he respected.

"I won't try to talk you out of it," he said. "But I want you to understand what you've meant to this place. We've had clients come to us specifically because your name was on the door. Not the firm's name. Yours. That doesn't happen often."

"I know," Cole said. "I'm sorry for the timing."

"Don't be." David was quiet for a moment. "You've given us ten good years. The work you did here — the Salish Sea project, the Meridian library, the Harborview commission — that's in the portfolio permanently. We benefit from that long after you're gone." He paused. "Wherever you land, it'll be better for having you. I mean that."

Cole didn't have an answer for that, so he just said thank you and meant it.

At four-thirty, Wren appeared at his door with a look that suggested she had been coordinating something he didn't know about. "Conference room," she said. "Just for a few minutes."

There was a cake — lemon, from the bakery two blocks over that everyone ordered from — and maybe fifteen people, some of whom Cole hadn't worked with closely in years. Marcus gave a short speech that was funny in the right places and didn't go on too long. Someone had found a photograph from the Friday Harbor project, Cole on the dock in rain gear, looking thoroughly pleased with himself, and had it printed and framed. He laughed when he saw it. He shook hands, accepted embraces, and promised to stay in touch, and he meant most of it.

He would miss them. That had never been the problem.

At five, as he was closing the box, Wren appeared in the doorway one more time. She set his mail on the corner of the desk — the last of it, neatly sorted — and picked up the coffee cup he'd left on the credenza.

"If you ever need an assistant," she said, "wherever you land — I hope you'll think of me."

He looked at her. "I will."

She nodded once and left.

By five he'd boxed the things that were his. Not many, as it turned out. He took his architecture degree and AIA membership certificate down from the wall and carefully placed them in the box. A site notebook from the Friday Harbor project. A scale rule he'd had since graduate school. A photograph of a small civic building in Bellingham — the first project he'd ever designed, since gutted and rebuilt by its current tenants. He took the Salish Sea Orca Center award down last. It was the only thing he'd been certain about taking.

He carried the box to his car and drove home through the last of the afternoon light. At some point, the road crossed above the water, and he found himself looking down at the canal rather than ahead — not from despair, just the old habit of reading a surface, wanting to understand what was moving underneath it. He hadn't known what he was looking for. He only knew he hadn't been finding it here for a long time.

He got home, set the box down in the entry, and stood in the quiet of his apartment.

He didn't know what came next. What he knew was that for the first time in years, that fact didn't frighten him.

Somewhere in the second week, he found himself standing in the lobby of his apartment building, a legal pad in hand, sketching a retrofit. The entry sequence was wrong — it processed people rather than welcoming them, a distinction the original architect had apparently never considered. The mailboxes were poorly placed, the lighting was institutional, and a wall that served no structural purpose was blocking what would have been a fine view of the courtyard. He spent four days on the drawings, then put together a cost estimate and a one-page summary. Then he took them to the building manager and explained what he had in mind.

She looked at the drawings for a long moment. "What does this cost?" she said.

"The construction? About what's on page two," Cole said. "I'm not charging for the design. I just live here." He turned to the summary. "If you raise rents fifty dollars a month across the building, you recover the construction cost in under two years. After that, it's margin."

She looked at him the way people sometimes did when he said something that didn't fit the expected shape of a conversation.

The lobby was renovated the following spring.

The call came three weeks after the resignation letter, from Patricia Huang, the chair of the Architecture Department at UW — a woman who had been two years ahead of Cole in graduate school and who had, as far as he knew, stayed in academia on purpose. She was matter-of-fact on the phone. The department ran a visiting lecture series on contemporary practice. Would Cole come talk to the graduate students about the Salish Sea project?

He said yes, mostly because he had nothing else scheduled.

The lecture hall held about eighty people. He'd expected a polite audience and gotten something else — students who argued with each other before he'd finished his sentences, who asked not about budget and schedule but about the acoustic modeling, about why the glass wall ran floor-to-ceiling rather than interrupted by structure, about whether the building changed when the tide went out. A student in the back row raised her hand and asked if you could hear the orcas from inside the building.

Cole had stopped. "I don't know," he'd said. "I never thought to check."

He went back the following week and checked. You could.

He'd expected forty-five minutes. The students kept him for ninety. When the room finally emptied, Patricia found him gathering his notes at the podium.

"You realize they stopped you," she said.

"I noticed."

She looked at him steadily. "We've been trying to build out a studio program specifically for practicing professionals — architects already working in the field who want to come back and deepen their practice. There's real demand for it, but we haven't had the right instructor. Someone who bridges both worlds." She paused. "Part-time. Full latitude on the projects. You'd be shaping the curriculum yourself."

He had been about to say he'd think about it.

"Yes," he said.

Catherine Thomas tracked him down a few weeks later. She'd heard about the resignation — she always heard — and she'd been waiting for the right moment.

They'd worked together years earlier on a small mixed-use building in Fremont that had come out exactly right. She'd trusted him then, and that trust had survived the decade in which she'd become a developer of consequence, and he'd become someone who counted the word "branding" in meetings. Now she sat across from him on Eastlake with a site plan rolled up beside her chair.

"Five stories," she said. "My own building. Glass, steel, warm wood. Live/work below, loft residences above. And I meant what I said years ago — if I ever built something of my own, I wanted you."

Cole unrolled the site plan and studied it. A corner lot at the north end of Lake Union, south-facing toward the water, the dimensions were generous without being excessive. He could feel the building's possibilities before he'd drawn a single line.

"I'll take it," he said.

By the time the penthouse was finished, teaching had become the steadiest thing in his week.

The fog sat on Lake Union like a held breath.

Cole walked the path from his building every morning when he was teaching — fifteen minutes along the north shore, past the houseboats riding low and dark in the grey water, the canal reduced to sound and impression. He'd taken the penthouse partly for this walk. The space itself was well-proportioned; his own design translated to his own life in a way that still surprised him some mornings. But it was the walk that had decided it — the knowledge that every teaching day would begin with the same fifteen-minute erasure of whatever had accumulated overnight.

The studio was on the third floor of Gould Hall. He arrived early enough to have the room to himself for a few minutes, standing at the windows with his coffee while the fog shifted over the water below.

Fifteen students were registered for the Advanced Design Studio for Practicing Professionals — a program Patricia had built around the gap Cole himself had just left. Half were mid-career architects returning to sharpen their practice; half were younger professionals who had been working long enough to know what questions they hadn't been taught to ask. The mix produced friction, and friction produced heat, and heat, occasionally, produced something worth watching.

He was midway through a desk critique — a student's residential scheme for a steeply sloped site in the Cascades — when it happened. Mei had designed something technically competent: a smart section, a clever structural response to the grade, good daylighting on the entry level. Cole had been working through it point by point when she stopped him.

"But what should it feel like?" she said. "When someone walks in. What should it feel like?"

Cole set down his pen.

He'd been at the firm for ten years. No client had ever asked that question. They asked about square footage, ceiling heights, and whether the kitchen island would photograph well for the listing. The investor committees asked about branding. No one asked what it should feel like.

"That's the right question," he said.

She blinked. "Yeah?"

"That's the only question. Everything else is in service of that."

He looked up. The other students had drifted closer without his noticing — fourteen people standing in a loose arc, everyone's own critique set aside. Cole reached for his iPad without thinking — the way he always did when an idea needed to move — and began sketching as he talked, shapes appearing and dissolving and reappearing in different forms. About the relationship between threshold and entry. About how a ceiling height prepares a body before the mind registers it. About restraint as a form of generosity — the building that doesn't insist, that lets the inhabitant feel at home rather than observed. About listening to a site the way you'd listen to a person: not for what they say first, but for what they say after that.

When he stopped, the room was quiet in a different way than before. Someone asked a question. Then another. He answered without checking himself, without performing. He couldn't remember the last time he'd felt this awake.

He walked home in the fog.

Weeks later, when Cole unrolled the plans across Catherine's conference table, she was quiet for a long moment.

"This is exactly right," she said.

"I know," Cole said.

She looked at him with the particular expression of someone who had learned to trust their own instincts and had just had that trust confirmed. "There's something else I want to talk to you about," she said. "The penthouse. Before anything is listed — you designed it, you get first choice."

He hadn't expected to say yes to that part. But when she took him through the unfinished shell — the concrete floor cold underfoot, the city visible through rough window openings on every side — something settled in him. The upper level stepped back from the roofline, a private space above the building's main volume with room for a deck and garden right outside tall glass doors facing south over the water. The elevator would open directly into the residence — no corridor, no shared floor, a key card the only passage between his world and the rest of the building. To someone else, it might have seemed extravagant. To Cole it was simpler than that: a place filled with light. A space where he could live and work and breathe.

He said yes.

The narrow lot adjacent to the building's south side had been on the market for years with no takers — more slope than lot, overgrown with blackberry and alder, tangled in floodplain restrictions that had defeated every owner who'd tried to build on it. The asking price reflected this history. Cole walked it three times before he said anything to Catherine.

He didn't want to build on it. He wanted to protect it.

The problem, when he sat down with it, turned out to have two faces. The subterranean garage ran along the building's south face —

three levels below grade — and its waterproofing had been engineered to strict tolerances. If the adjacent slope's drainage changed, even subtly, the water behavior beneath grade would change with it. Touch the lot's grade, and you affected the garage. Leave the drainage alone and you accepted limits on how the path could run. The two problems were the same problem.

He had a habit, when something refused to resolve itself in words, of drawing it into a shape he could look at. Not architectural drawings — something more private and provisional, a visual language he'd developed over the years that would have meant nothing to anyone else. He sat at the drafting table he'd wedged into the spare room and opened his iPad and began: WP in a rectangle at the top, SG below it, DR curving down the left margin, arrows indicating flow and grade and sequence, question marks nested inside other question marks. G-lvl. Perc-rate? Cut or fill? The shapes accumulated across the screen in clusters — a map of the problem's interior that only made sense from where he was sitting.

He filled two screens before he saw it. The path had to stay high — not cutting toward the canal directly, but curving north first, following the slope's longest natural axis before turning south toward the water. That alignment kept it entirely above the drainage threshold. The water could move the way it had always moved, away from the garage's footprint, along the grade's original logic.

The longer curve was the better path. The problem had been pointing at the design the whole time.

He brought a quiet sketch to the city: native vegetation, a decomposed-granite path following the natural grade, no new runoff, no new loads on the infrastructure. A natural open space that met the slope on its own terms and connected, at the lower edge, to the canal trail. The city responded better than he'd hoped.

He went to Catherine with the idea plainly: if she'd acquire the lot and donate it to the city, he'd design the open space at no charge and treat both sites — the building and the ground beside it — as a single vision.

She said yes.

Standing on the slope afterward, sketching the path alignment in the failing light, Cole felt something he hadn't felt in a long time. Not pride. Something quieter and more specific: alignment. The sense that what he was doing and who he was were pointing in the same direction.

He hadn't known the work could still feel like this.

2

ABOUT FACE

The call came from Mike Danner on a Tuesday morning in August — a voice Cole didn't know, unhurried and direct, identifying itself without preamble. Catherine Thomas had given him the number. He had a property on Hood Canal. He wasn't looking for a contractor or a project manager. He was looking for someone who could see what a place wanted to be.

Cole said he could come look.

The ferry left Colman Dock at seven-forty. Cole arrived early enough to drive onto the car deck without hurrying, then went up to the passenger level while the dock lines were still being cast off. The terminal fell away. Seattle's waterfront slid past and then opened into the grey expanse of the Sound, the Olympic Peninsula a low blue suggestion at the far edge of visibility.

He got a coffee from the galley and took it out to the upper deck. The engines were a low vibration underfoot, the bow wave creaming away below him in two clean lines. The morning was clear and still, the kind of August day the Pacific Northwest holds in reserve for when it wants to remind you why you live here. The Olympics rose clean and white to the west, their snowfields brilliant in the early light. The water was deep blue and nearly flat, catching the sun in long, slow facets. A harbor seal surfaced briefly off the port bow, considered the ferry with apparent indifference, and was gone. He had brought nothing but his iPad and a habit of looking.

He drove off in Bremerton into full sun. The town gave way quickly — a few miles of commercial strip, then the road moved south through the peninsula in a long corridor of fir and cedar, the development thinning until there was nothing but trees and the occasional turnoff with a hand-lettered sign.

He passed a small motel near one of the highway junctions — a low row of rooms with a hand-lettered sign missing its second 'l', a vending machine visible through a screen door, a parking lot with three cars and a boat trailer. A paper banner in the office window read VACANCY. It was the kind of place that had served this corridor for decades without aspiring to be anything other than dry and affordable, and Cole didn't fault it for that. He just noticed it. There was nothing else to stop for between here and wherever Mike Danner was waiting.

The road eventually bent west along the south shore of the canal, and Hood Canal appeared through the trees on his right and didn't leave again. He followed it north on the highway, the water opening and closing between the firs, until the roads grew smaller and quieter with each turn.

He pulled over and stopped. The water was deep and still in the August light, the far shore close enough to read the treeline but distant enough to feel like another world. A great blue heron stood motionless at the waterline below the road, attending to something Cole couldn't see.

He sat for a moment, then pulled back onto the road.

The Lodge sat at the end of a gravel drive that curved around a stand of western hemlocks, revealing the building only at the last moment. When he got out of the car, the air came at him all at once — salt and wet fir bark and something green underneath, the smell of a coast that had been doing this for a very long time. Cole stopped the car and studied it through the windshield. Low and dark, with a roofline that seemed to press downward rather than lift, the building hunkered against the hillside as though trying to disappear into it. The walls were board-and-batten siding gone almost black with moisture and age, the wood swollen in places, moss colonizing the lower courses where the grade had settled and pooled. The windows were small — punched-hole openings that admitted light grudgingly, more like gaps than views — and the entry door faced the parking area, its back to the cove, as though placed by someone who had forgotten which way the water was. Or perhaps never thought to ask. Thirty yards through the trees, Hood Canal sat brilliant in the August sun, entirely ignored.

He got out of the car.

Mike Danner came around the side of the building before Cole had taken three steps — a broad-shouldered man in his mid-fifties with work-roughened hands and the unhurried manner of someone who had long ago made peace with the pace of things. He didn't offer a handshake immediately. He looked at Cole the way Cole had been looking at the building.

"You saw it right away," Mike said. "The building's facing the wrong direction."

"Yes," Cole said.

Mike nodded, as though this confirmed something he'd been waiting to hear. "Come on," he said. "Let me show you what I've got."

The front door opened inward with the particular resistance of a door that had swelled in its frame and been forced so many times that the latch no longer caught properly. Mike held it without comment. Cole stepped through.

His eyes adjusted slowly. The entry was a dim, low-ceilinged space that smelled of wood damp and something older beneath it — decades of fires in a poorly drawing fireplace, cooking grease worked into the walls, the accumulated presence of guests who had stayed here because it was available and not because it was good. A bare bulb above the front desk cast a yellow circle on the paneled wall behind it. The paneling was dark-stained pine, tongue-and-groove, run floor to ceiling on every surface, the kind of interior decision that had seemed warm once and now simply absorbed what little light there was.

Cole moved through the space without speaking. He had learned early that buildings told you more before you started asking questions.

The common room was larger, which made the low ceiling feel worse. A stone fireplace occupied the interior wall — the wrong wall, Cole noted, its back to the water — and the furniture was arranged around it in the permanent crouch of a room that had given up on the view. Two windows faced the cove. They were small, single-paned, set high in the wall as though the original builder had thought of light as something to be rationed rather than invited. Through them, between the hemlocks, Cole could see a thin strip of grey water. Hood Canal, thirty yards away, visible only in glimpses, as something glimpsed through a closing door.

"How many rooms?" Cole asked.

"Twelve," Mike said. "Six on each side of the hall." He paused. "All facing the parking area."

He said it the way someone names a thing they've long since stopped being surprised by. Cole glanced at him. There was no apology in it, and no embarrassment — just the plain statement of someone who had lived with an inherited problem long enough to see it clearly.

They walked the hall. The guest rooms were small and identical: a window that faced the gravel, a bed, and a narrow bathroom tiled in beige. Each room felt like it had been designed to provide the minimum conditions for sleep and nothing more. Cole stood in the last doorway for a moment, looking at the window — at the parking area, at the hemlocks, at the complete absence of water — and felt the waste of it settle over him like weather.

"Come around back," Mike said.

They went out through a side door and around the building's rear. The change was immediate. The hemlocks thinned, the grade dropped slightly toward the water, and the cove opened before them — a quiet, enclosed arm of Hood Canal, perhaps three hundred yards across, the far shore a dark line of fir against the August sky. The water was very still. A great blue heron stood motionless at the far edge of a gravel bar, its patience total.

Cole stood without speaking for a long moment.

The building's back wall was directly behind him — blank board-and-batten, no windows, no door, no acknowledgment that this existed. Thirty feet of overgrown grass separated the structure from the water's edge. He turned and looked at the wall, then turned back to the cove.

"This is what you've got," he said.

"This is what I've got," Mike agreed.

Mike was quiet for a moment, his hands in his pockets. Then, almost apologetically: "This isn't right. A place like this shouldn't hide. It needs to feel open to the fjord and part of it — not closed off, as if someone was afraid to let the light in. People should walk in here and breathe easier, not squint to see where they're going. Families should sit down and feel the cove around them. Feel the light move. Feel the tide change." He let out a slow breath. "A place that gives more than it takes away. That's what this should be. This place should belong to the landscape, not shut it out."

Cole didn't speak at first. Mike spoke in instinct; Cole heard the architecture beneath it. The orientation flipping toward the water. The volume opening. The windows widening until the fjord could finally breathe through the structure instead of around it.

Cole looked at the blank wall again. Then at the water. The cove was sheltered and still, the light on its surface shifting in slow, barely perceptible patterns — the kind of light that changed everything depending on the hour, the season, the weather. He thought about what these rooms could be if they faced this instead of a parking lot. He thought about glass — not windows but walls — and the threshold between inside and outside dissolving entirely. He thought about waking up in this place and what it would mean to have the water be the first thing you saw.

He recognized the feeling. It was the same one he'd had standing over the tidal flats in Friday Harbor, before a single line had been drawn. The sense of a building that didn't exist yet pulling him toward it.

"There's more to it than what you can see from here," Mike added quietly. "The cove. What's in it. You'd have to spend some time here to understand."

He reached for his iPad, then stopped. "How many rooms are you thinking?"

Mike looked at the water for a moment. "Right now we have twenty-two. I'd like to get to fifty. Rooms, suites, cottages — a mix. Something for different kinds of guests." He paused, "We close the last week of September. I'd need to be open by Memorial Day weekend. Eight months." He said it plainly, without apology, the way a man states a fact he's already made peace with.

Cole looked at him. "That's quite a challenge."

Mike held his gaze. "I know."

Cole turned to look at the bluff rising behind the property, then back at the waterline, then at the Lodge's blank rear wall. "I'm not thinking about rooms off a corridor," he said. "The Lodge itself becomes the communal heart — restaurant, gathering spaces, the great room — all of it reoriented toward the water, opened to the cove. The guest rooms are entirely outside the building. Small buildings in the trees — three, four rooms each — fitted into the hillside wherever the landscape allows it. Some down near the water, some among the hemlocks, some up the bluff. Each cluster finding its own site. Private. Quiet. Guests wouldn't be staying in a lodge — they'd be staying in the landscape, with the Lodge as the place they come together."

He stopped and looked at Mike.

Mike was quiet for a long moment, his eyes moving slowly across the property the way Cole's had — the bluff, the tree line, the water. He didn't object. He didn't ask about cost, schedule or whether it was feasible. He just nodded once, as though Cole had said something he'd been waiting to hear.

That was what decided it.

He opened his iPad.

Cole came back the following Tuesday.

He'd spent the week between visits doing what he always did after the first walk-through of a project: nothing. Or what looked like nothing — long walks in the early morning, his iPad on the kitchen table with nothing on it, the site plan from the county assessor's office taped to the wall of the spare room where he could look at it while making coffee. The design hadn't started yet. What he was doing was listening.

By Tuesday, he was ready to ask questions.

Mike met him in the gravel lot, shook his hand, and walked him toward the Lodge's side entry. "There's someone you need to know," he said. "Sam Westhill. She runs this place. Has for years. She knows every inch of it — the rooms, the kitchen, the way guests move through on a Friday afternoon when there's a wedding. She'll tell you things about this building I can't." He paused at the door. "I mean that literally. Sam knows this place better than I do."

He pushed the door open, let Cole through first, and then — with the easy confidence of a man who trusts absolutely what he's set in motion — walked back toward the parking area and disappeared around the corner.

Cole stood in the side hallway.

Sam Westhill was behind the front desk with a printed reservation ledger open in front of her, making notes in the margins in a hand that suggested she didn't expect anyone else to read it. She was in her late twenties, compact and self-contained, with the watchful stillness of someone who had learned early that paying close attention was its own form of protection. She looked up at Cole with an expression that was professionally neutral in a way that wasn't neutral at all.

"Cole Walker," she said. Not a question.

"Yes."

She closed the ledger. "Mike said you'd come back on Tuesday." She came around the desk with a clipboard. "I've got four hours before I have a call with our linen vendor. Where do you want to start?"

"Service flow," Cole said. "How does the back of house work — laundry, linen, deliveries. Where things enter and where they go."

A pause — brief, almost imperceptible. "Most architects want to start with the views."

"I'll get to the views," Cole said.

She looked at him for a moment. Then: "Follow me."

She walked him through the service corridor first — a narrow passage running along the building's interior spine, half the width it needed to be, with a linen closet at one end that had been retrofitted into a bathroom at some point, shifting the storage to an outbuilding forty yards from the nearest guest room. Cole asked how housekeeping managed the distance. She told him. He asked about the peak laundry load on a Saturday. She told him that, too. He drew neither the corridor nor the outbuilding. He drew the path between them, marked with an arrow and a number.

"That's not on any plan I've seen," she said.

"It's not a plan yet," Cole said. "It's a problem."

She said nothing. They kept moving.

The kitchen was at the back of the building, facing — of course — the parking area. A man Cole hadn't met was at the prep counter with

his back to the door, working through a stack of leeks with the focused efficiency of someone who had not invited observation and didn't intend to welcome it.

"Louis," Sam said.

"Je sais," the man said, without turning around.

Sam glanced at Cole as if to say: you're on your own. Then she stepped back to examine something on the far wall.

Cole walked to the pass-through window — a standard hotel arrangement, nothing special — and looked through it toward where the dining room would be. "How many covers on a Saturday in August?" he asked.

Louis set down his knife. He turned slowly, with the precise economy of someone who had calculated exactly how much movement the situation required. He was in his early forties, compact and unhurried, and he looked at Cole the way he might look at a delivery he hadn't ordered.

"Devinez," he said. Then, seeing Cole's expression: "Guess."

Cole thought for a moment. "Eighty."

Louis picked up his knife again. "One hundred thirty. Come back when you have thought about it."

They came out through the kitchen's service door onto the gravel apron behind the building. The cove was right there — thirty yards of overgrown grass and then the water, flat and still in the afternoon light. Sam didn't stop. She walked him down the slope toward the waterline, the gravel giving way to a worn path through salal and sword fern.

At the water's edge, she stopped. The cove was quiet. Eelgrass showed dark through the shallows, moving in slow undulations with the current.

"When you start construction," Sam said, "what happens to that?"

Cole looked at the eelgrass. Then at her.

"Silt," she said. "You tear up the grade above the waterline, you get runoff. Runoff carries sediment into the cove. Sediment smothers eelgrass. Eelgrass is a nursery habitat — juvenile salmon shelter in it. Juvenile salmon feed the adults. The adults feed the orcas." She looked at him steadily. "So when your crew is up there regrading the site, and the first rain comes, what kind of erosion controls are you planning?"

She said it the way she'd said everything that afternoon — professionally, without hostility — but there was something underneath it now. A line she'd drawn. This was not about the service corridor, the linen closet, or Louis's covers on a Saturday. This was about what she actually cared about.

Cole was quiet for a moment. He looked at the eelgrass, at the gravel bar where it thinned, at the slope behind them where the grade would have to change.

"How far does the eelgrass extend?" he asked. "Along the shoreline."

It was not the answer she'd expected. She told him. He asked about the current pattern through the cove, and she told him that too. He drew neither the eelgrass nor the current. He drew the slope above the waterline and marked where the runoff would concentrate in heavy rain.

Sam watched him work. She didn't say anything else. She didn't need to. He'd heard her.

They were crossing the side lot on the way back toward the Lodge entrance when Cole noticed the man standing beside the groundskeeping shed. Tall, early thirties, with the loose posture of someone who had mastered the art of appearing occupied without doing anything. He was leaning against the shed wall with his phone in one hand and a work glove on the other, as though he had been about to do something and had decided, upon reflection, not to.

"Trevor," Sam said, without slowing. "The paving stones along the east path need to be reset before we close."

"I know," Trevor Maddox said.

She kept walking. Cole kept pace.

"Mike's nephew," she said quietly, once they were past. "Groundskeeping superintendent."

She didn't say anything else. She didn't need to.

3

A NEW VIEW

The last guests checked out on a Saturday morning in late September. By noon the parking area was empty, the gravel raked clean by the wind, and the Lodge stood quiet for the first time in months.

Mike gathered the staff in the common room at two o'clock. Fourteen people — housekeeping, front desk, kitchen, grounds — arranged in a loose half-circle in the low-ceilinged space that had been the center of this place for as long as most of them had worked here. The fireplace was cold. The paneled walls absorbed what little afternoon light came through the small windows. It was, as it had always been, a room that asked nothing of you and gave nothing back.

Mike stood at the front of it without notes.

"I'm not going to make this long," he said. "You know what's happening. We're closing for the season — longer than usual. Eight months, maybe nine. When we come back, the building you're standing in won't be here anymore. What replaces it will be worth the wait. I believe that." He paused. "I want every one of you back in the spring. Everyone. And I'm going to make sure you're taken care of while we're closed. Sam has the details, and she'll sit down with each of you individually. But I didn't want that to be the first thing I said. The first thing I wanted to say is thank you."

He said it the way he said most things — plainly, without decoration, meaning it completely.

The room was quiet. Someone near the back — one of the housekeeping staff, a woman who'd been making beds in this building for eleven years — started crying quietly and then stopped herself. Louis Beaumont stood with his arms folded and his eyes on the middle distance, his expression unreadable in the particular way of a man who feels things precisely and chooses carefully when to show it.

Trevor Maddox stood at the edge of the group near the door, his phone in his jacket pocket. He'd been there when Mike started, and he was still there now, which, Sam reflected, was more than she'd expected.

Mike took questions for a few minutes — practical ones, about timing, references, and whether the spring opening date was firm. He answered each one directly. When there were no more questions, he thanked them again, and the room began to empty in the quiet, slightly stunned way of gatherings that have ended but haven't quite finished.

Sam stayed until everyone else had gone. Mike was standing at the window — one of the small, grudging windows that faced the parking area — looking out at nothing in particular.

"You doing all right?" she said.

"Yeah," he said. He didn't turn around. "You?"

"Asking me to come back to a building I actually want to work in?" She picked up her jacket from the chair. "I'll manage."

He almost smiled. She left him there with the window and the quiet and whatever he needed to finish before he could walk out.

Cole brought the plans to the construction trailer that afternoon. Rain had been coming in off the canal since morning, loud on the thin metal roof in a way the finished Lodge never would be. Mike was already there. Sam came in from the office with a notebook and leaned against the counter with her arms folded — the posture she used when she intended to listen carefully and say very little until she had something worth saying.

Cole unrolled the site plan and started with the Lodge itself — the reorientation toward the water, the great room, the restaurant, the glass fronts. Then he moved to the second sheet.

"The guest buildings," he said. "Two stories, but you'd never know it from the path. You walk in at grade to a common room — that's the upper level. Bedrooms step down the slope below, glass fronts facing the water. Decks on both levels. The hemlocks don't branch until sixty, seventy feet up — both decks are under the canopy, looking through the understory to the cove. You're in the forest at both levels. Smaller footprint on the ground, less disruption to the root systems."

"That's a lot of ground for housekeeping to cover," Sam said. "In the rain."

"Each building has a utility closet on the upper level," Cole said. "Linens, towels, cleaning supplies, vacuum — everything housekeeping needs is already there. Staff walk between buildings carrying nothing." He traced a line on the plan. "A paved service path connects them along the hillside — permeable pavers, same as the drive. Wide enough for an electric golf cart. Quiet. Doesn't break the atmosphere."

Sam unfolded her arms slightly.

"The cart handles restocking, deliveries, room service," Cole continued. "Heated and cooled compartments — food arrives at the right temperature, wine stays cold." He glanced at Sam. "If Louis is sending a dinner up the hill, it gets there the way he'd want it to get there."

Mike looked at Sam. Sam looked at Mike.

"A few of the buildings at the base of the hill are single-story," Cole said. "ADA accessible. Flat entry from the path, no stairs, wider doorways, roll-in showers. Close to the Lodge, so the path runs level." He paused. "Older guests, families with strollers, anyone who needs it. They shouldn't have to ask for a workaround."

Sam was quiet for a moment. Then: "You've really put a lot of thought into this."

"It's what I do," Cole said.

The morning after the last guest left, Cole unrolled the site plans on the hood of his truck. Sam found him there on her way to the office — drawings weighted with coffee mugs, the replacement dock plan on top.

She stopped. Looked at it.

"Walk with me," she said.

They went down to the dock. The old structure creaked under their weight — grey planking, rail bolts rusted to orange, the pilings driven straight out from shore into the cove. Dock lines ran from cleats worn smooth by years of handling, down to a pair of skiffs that rode the slow pull of the tide. It had been there for decades. It worked. Nobody had ever questioned where it was.

Sam crouched at the edge and pointed into the shallows. "See the eelgrass?" Dark shapes moved in slow undulations just below the surface, running along the shoreline on either side of the dock. "The current carries nutrients along the shore and through the beds. The pilings cut right across that flow — they create turbulence and push sediment into the beds on the far side." She pointed past the last piling. "The nursery habitat starts just beyond the end. Juvenile salmon shelter there. Every tide change, these pilings send a pulse of disruption straight through it."

She stood up. "Your replacement plan has the new pilings in the same line."

Cole looked at the plan in his hand. Looked at the water. Looked at the pilings.

He tore the page in half.

"Then we won't do that," he said.

They watched from the bluff.

Before the demolition contractor arrived, a salvage crew had spent three days inside the building pulling timber. The Lodge's exposed interior beams — old-growth Douglas fir, secondary structural and decorative elements the crew could remove without compromising the frame, some of them fourteen inches across and dense in the way that wood only gets with age — were worth more than the structure around them. The crew moved carefully, cutting them free section by section and carrying them out to the parking area where they were stacked and wrapped against the weather. Cole had been on site for part of it, moving through the gutted interior with his iPad, making notes. Several of the longest spans he'd already drawn back into the new Lodge's design. The wood that had held this building up for decades would hold the new one, too — visible this time, appreciated, doing what it had always been capable of.

On the second afternoon of the salvage, when a section of the interior wall on the cove-facing side came down, Mike was there. For a moment, through the opened frame, the full width of the cove appeared — bright water in the afternoon light, unobstructed, closer than it had ever seemed from inside the building. He stood in the gap for a long time without saying anything to anyone. Then he went back to what he'd been doing.

A demolition contractor had spent two days wiring the charges after the salvage was done — a quiet, methodical man who moved through the stripped shell with the deliberate patience of someone defusing something rather than destroying it, threading det cord through the walls and along the base of the remaining posts, marking each connection with a numbered tag. Mike had watched him work for an hour the first morning and then left him to it. Some things you commission and then let be.

Now Mike and Sam stood above the tree line with their coffee, watching from the bluff near their cottages as the contractor's crew cleared the perimeter and the radio crackled through its final checks.

The morning was still. Hood Canal lay flat and silver behind the building, the October light low and clean. The Lodge sat where it had always sat — dark, compact, its back to the water as though it had never learned which direction mattered.

Cole stood in the parking area below, hands in his jacket pockets, keeping his distance. He'd been on this site for weeks now. The building coming down was not his moment to stand close to.

The warning horn sounded twice.

A voice came over the loudspeaker — flat, unhurried, the voice of a man who had done this many times. "Ten. Nine. Eight." Sam set down her coffee. "Seven. Six. Five." Mike didn't move. "Four. Three. Two. One."

Then the charges went — a sharp, sequential percussion, almost too fast to follow — and the Lodge dropped straight down into itself, the walls folding inward and the roof riding the collapse all the way to the ground. A beat of silence. Then the fire crews moved in — two trucks that had been staged on the cove side of the perimeter, the men up the ladders before the dust had cleared the roofline, the hoses arcing down into the cloud from above. What should have rolled across the hillside and out over the water went nowhere. It fell back heavy and wet across the rubble, settling into itself.

When it cleared, there was nothing. A low heap of timber and siding, already smaller than it had any right to be. And beyond it, unobstructed for the first time in anyone's memory, the full sweep of the cove — the water bright and still, the far shore dark with fir, the morning light doing exactly what it had always wanted to do with that view.

Mike stood with his mug in both hands and said nothing for a long moment.

Sam stood beside him and felt something she hadn't quite expected: relief.

She'd worked in that building for over a decade. Every stuck door, every dim hallway, every cold corner where the insulation had long since given up. Low ceilings, small windows, the light rationed like something precious and scarce. She'd never said it out loud, but the place had always felt slightly airless — designed by someone who thought comfort meant enclosure. A dungeon with amenities. And now it was a pile of grey boards and a view.

"I'm not going to miss it," she said.

Mike glanced at her. "No?"

"Always felt like I needed to duck."

He was quiet for a moment. Then, mildly: "The ceilings were nine feet."

"I know what they were," Sam said.

He almost smiled. "Had it since I was young," he said, not quite to her. "Strange thing to watch."

Sam said nothing. She understood it wasn't the same as regret.

Mike looked at the cove for a long moment — at the light on the water, at the space where the building had been, at all of it finally visible. "There it is," he said.

"About time," Sam said;

He was the first one on the grounds that morning, earlier than he'd meant to be, coffee in hand, picking his way through the debris field where the east wing had stood the day before. The demolition crew had been efficient — what had taken thirty years to settle into the hillside took six hours to come apart. What remained was a wide gap in the Lodge's footprint, open sky where the roofline had been, the smell of old wood and cold air.

He heard them before he saw them. A low movement in the tree line, branches adjusting, and then the first one stepped through — a cow elk, unhurried, reading the changed landscape with her nose. The others followed. He stopped and held still. A herd of maybe fifteen, moving in the loose, purposeful way of animals that have been crossing this ground since before the Lodge existed. They filtered through the open gap, through the space that had been someone's dining room, through the place where the new framing would start going up in a matter of hours.

Then the bull came through last, and Cole understood immediately why people stepped back. He'd seen elk at a distance, assumed he had the scale of them. He didn't. The animal was enormous in a way that rearranged the space around it — heavy-shouldered, deliberate, its rack clearing the surrounding scrub with a kind of unhurried authority. It paused and looked at Cole directly, sizing him up and apparently finding nothing worth further attention, and moved on.

They were gone in a few minutes. Cole stood a little longer, looking at where they'd been, his coffee going cold in his hand.

One evening at the construction trailer, Cole spread the site circulation plan across the table and walked Mike through it. The day-trip divers were the problem — they needed the water but not the Lodge, and without a clear path in they'd come through the front door. Cole had drawn a roundabout with three spokes: one to the back of the Dive Shop, where day divers would drop gear at a service window and collect keycards; one up to the guest buildings, gated; one into the forest to the staff cottages, gated. Day divers would park in the main lot and walk to the East Gate — keycard entry to the Dive Shop complex. The gate logged every transit: timestamp, card ID, direction.

Mike studied it. "They drop their gear, and the gate keeps them out of the hotel."

"And keeps guests from wandering into a dive staging area," Cole said. "Same problem, same solution."

Mike nodded once, and they moved on to the next sheet.

That same week, Cole caught a flatbed parked on the root zone of a Western hemlock near the west lawn. He was at the driver's door before the engine was off.

"Move the truck," Cole said.

The driver looked at him. "There's nowhere else to — "

"These trees have been here for over a thousand years. Since before the Norman Invasion." Cole pointed at the ground beneath the wheels. "The root system is right there, just under the surface. You park on it, you compact the soil, and you kill what twelve centuries couldn't." He stepped back. "Move the truck."

The truck moved. The fencing went up the next morning — orange plastic web staked around the drip line of every mature hemlock and Douglas fir on the property.

Walking the hillside to site the guest buildings, Cole realized the orange web had mapped the answer for him — the root zones showed where you couldn't build, and the gaps between them showed where you could.

It wasn't one thing. It was the way Garrett answered questions.

Cole had been on enough job sites to know the difference between a contractor who was busy and a contractor who was managing you. Garrett Holt was never quite available when Cole wanted to look at something, always just finishing a call or needed elsewhere, always with an answer that came a half-second too quickly and moved a half-step too far from the specific question asked. Cole had logged it the way he logged everything — without comment, in a corner of his notebook no one else would see.

He'd arranged his teaching schedule around it — both studios back to back, Tuesdays and Wednesdays, so the drive happened once in each direction instead of twice. The rest of the week belonged to Hood Canal.

The foundation pour was the third week of October. Cole was on site when Garrett arrived to walk through the mix design — the spec, the slump targets, the curing plan for the overnight temperatures already dropping toward freezing. It was a routine pre-pour conversation. Garrett ran through it without hesitation, hitting every point in the right order, the language fluent and precise. He'd clearly done this a hundred times.

Cole listened and said nothing he wouldn't have said on any other job. But something was off. He couldn't have named it — not yet. It wasn't a number or a claim he could point to. It was a quality in the answers: too complete, like a prepared statement. Garrett was giving him what he'd come to give, not what the questions had drawn out. The difference was small. Cole had learned not to dismiss small.

Cole walked it the morning after with the site foreman, asking the usual questions about cure time and blanket placement for the overnight temperatures. The answers were fine. The concrete looked fine. He stood at the edge of the formed slab and felt the unease he'd learned, over twenty years, not to argue with.

He called a materials testing firm in Bremerton that afternoon. Independent, no connection to the project. He asked for core samples from three locations and a full compression test series. He said nothing to Mike, nothing to Garrett, nothing to Sam. He waited.

The results came back ten days later. Two of the three cores tested below the specified compressive strength — not by a catastrophic margin, but enough. Enough to matter in a structure built on a bluff above tidal water. Enough to matter in twenty years when the loads shifted, and the freeze-thaw cycles had done their work. Enough.

Cole called Mike that evening. "I need you at the site tomorrow morning," he said. "Eight o'clock. And I'd like Garrett there as well."

Mike was quiet for a moment. "Should I know what this is about?"

"Yes," Cole said, and told him.

Garrett arrived at eight-ten, unhurried, with the ease of a man who hadn't yet understood what kind of morning this was going to be. Cole was standing at the foundation with the test report in his hand. Mike stood a few feet back, hands in his jacket pockets, saying nothing.

Cole handed Garrett the report. Gave him time to read it.

"This is one firm's results," Garrett said. "Lab error happens. I'd want my own testing before we — "

"Two of three cores," Cole said. "Same deficiency in both. That's not a lab error. That's a pattern." He took the report back and turned to the data page. "Spec called for four thousand PSI at twenty-eight days. You're at thirty-two hundred in the northeast section, thirty-four in the southwest. You want to tell me how a lab manages to be consistently wrong in the same direction across two separate samples?"

Garrett said nothing.

"I'll tell you what happened," Cole said. "The mix came off the truck too stiff for your crew to work it the way they wanted, so somebody added water on site. Probably more than once. You raise the water-cement ratio, and you get workability, and you lose strength, and if nobody tests it, nobody knows. That's the calculation you made." He paused. "Am I wrong?"

Garrett looked at the foundation. "Conditions on site that day — "

"Am I wrong?"

A long moment. "The numbers are what they are," Garrett said finally. "But we're talking about a lodge, not a hospital. The loading on this slab — "

"Don't." The word landed flat and final, and something in Cole's voice had shifted — the vowels flattened and slowed, the Pacific Northwest ironed out of them, something older and more deliberate underneath. "This building is going on a bluff above tidal water, and it is going to stand there for fifty years through freeze-thaw cycles and lateral loads and every storm that comes off that canal. You don't get to decide what margin of error is acceptable on somebody else's building. That is not a decision that belongs to you."

The accent was fully out now — unhurried and unambiguous, each word given its full weight. Cole wasn't shouting. He was, if anything, quieter than before. That was, Garrett seemed to be realizing, the wrong sign.

"You're going to remove the affected sections and repour to spec," Cole said. "At your cost. Not Mike's. Yours. There will be no change order — this is not a change. This is you doing what you contracted to do and didn't. And you're going to let my testing firm verify the new pours before we proceed. If that's not something you're willing to do, then we're done here, and Mike can decide what comes next." He paused. "I'd think carefully before you answer."

Garrett thought carefully. He agreed.

After he'd gone, Mike stood looking at the foundation for a long moment without speaking. Cole was making notes in his site book, the pen moving in short, deliberate strokes.

"Where are you from?" Mike said.

Cole looked up. "North Carolina."

Mike nodded slowly, as though this explained several things at once. "That's a hundred thousand dollars you just saved me. Minimum."

"You hired me to look after your building," Cole said. "That's what I'm doing."

He went back to his notes. Mike watched him for another moment, then walked back toward the Lodge. He was smiling, though Cole didn't see it.

Mike found Sam in the office that afternoon, a coursework window open on one side of her screen and the spring reopening reservation calendar on the other. She'd been taking Resort Management classes part-time for five years, fitting them around the Lodge's seasons, and when the closure was confirmed, she'd registered full-time before the end of the week. Her decision, start to finish. He sat down across from her without preamble and told her what had happened — the test results, the PSI numbers, the conversation with Garrett. He told it plainly, the way he told most things, without commentary or conclusion. Then he got up and went back outside.

Sam sat with it for a while after he left.

She'd been certain about Cole Walker from the moment Mike had described him: another architect with a portfolio and a vision and no real interest in how a working lodge actually functioned. She'd been polite because Mike asked it of her and because she was professional, but she'd been waiting — patiently, with considerable experience on her side — for the moment when he'd prove her right.

He hadn't ordered the testing because Mike had asked him to. He hadn't done it to impress anyone. He'd done it because something hadn't felt right to him, and he'd followed that feeling quietly and alone until he had something real to stand on. And then he'd stood on it.

She looked out the window at the construction site, at the foundation that would now be what it was supposed to be, and she allowed herself the small, uncomfortable thought that she might have had him wrong from the start.

She didn't say anything to anyone. But she stopped waiting for him to fail.

4

FROM THE RIGHT DEPTH

Sam's cottage was small and lit warmly, the table already set when Cole arrived. A fire had been going earlier — the smell of woodsmoke still in the room, faint and pleasant. The food had come from Louis's kitchen — pasta, a salad, bread still warm from the oven — carried up the hill in covered dishes the way Louis occasionally did for the staff, without comment or explanation, as though feeding people was simply a condition of his existence.

Claire was already there. Sam introduced them without ceremony. "This is Claire. We're getting married in July." Claire was a vet with a clinic in Hoodsport. She had the kind of stillness that comes from spending time with animals: attentive without being intrusive, present without performing it.

They ate. The conversation moved easily — the construction schedule, the retractable roof system Cole was still refining, a brief argument between Sam and Claire about whether the otters in the cove were the same two from last summer or new ones. Claire said yes. Sam said no. Neither of them had evidence. Cole found himself talking more than he usually did. Something about the table made it easy.

He was midway through describing the light in the framing — the way the morning slid across the structural ribs, the particular quality of it that had started to feel like a reason rather than a coincidence — when Claire set down her fork.

"You left a job you didn't like," she said, "because it was making you forget why you wanted to build things."

Cole stopped.

He glanced at Sam.

"I didn't tell her that," Sam said.

"You didn't have to," Claire said. "It's in the way you talk about the Lodge. Like you're remembering something instead of making something up."

She said it without weight, the way you'd note the tide was going out. Then she picked up her fork, and the conversation moved on.

Later, after Claire had gone to bed — six o'clock start at the clinic, she said, as a fact rather than an apology — Sam poured coffee and sat back down at the table.

"She does that," Sam said. "Sees things. I don't know how."

"She's right, though," Cole said.

"She always is." A pause. "That's the terrifying part."

The coffee was good. Outside, the cove was dark and quiet. Somewhere across the water, a boat's engine turned over and ran for a minute, then went still — the sound carried with perfect clarity in the cold air.

Sam turned her cup in her hands. "I didn't think you'd listen," she said. "The eelgrass. The dock. The cove. Most consultants hear it, nod, and do what they were going to do anyway."

Cole looked at her. "You were right," he said. "Every time."

"I know," Sam said. "That's what I'm telling you."

The following week it rained every day, steady and cold, the kind of rain that soaked into the lumber and turned the site to mud. The crew worked through it without complaint. The framing was up by early November.

The air on the site had changed — fresh-cut Douglas fir, the smell of it sharp and clean in the cold. Ravens had been working the perimeter since the first beam went up; the eagles came a week later, two of them settling on the top plates as if they'd always been there, watching Cole cross the site with the particular patience of birds that knew they had the better view.

Some mornings, walking the site before first light, he'd hear owls calling back and forth across the cove, their voices carrying through the hemlock stand with an ease that made the dark feel smaller. One morning one came through without a sound — a shape crossing the open framing two feet from his face, there and gone before he could react. His heart was going before he understood what he'd seen.

Cole walked the framing most mornings before the crew arrived, reading the structure the way he always did at this stage — not looking at what was there, but listening for what wasn't.

Something was missing at the center. He could feel it in the framing — a void where the building wanted to open but hadn't been told how. He'd brought three different proposals to Mike over the past several weeks: a skylight system, a clerestory running the length of the ridge line, and a glazed cupola. Each one technically sound. Each one solving the problem of light at the building's core. Mike had looked at each one carefully, asked questions, and said the same thing.

"Not yet."

Not too expensive. Not wrong. Just — not yet. No explanation.

Cole had pushed back the third time. "The building needs this. The interior will be dark at its center, with no significant light feature. You can see it in the framing."

"I can see it," Mike said. "Not yet."

Cole let it go because Mike had earned that much. But he didn't understand.

One morning, as they walked the site, Mike paused at the edge of the bluff. The tide was low, the cove below them quiet. He stood there a moment, not checking anything, just looking at the water.

"You ever dive?" he asked.

Cole shook his head. "No."

"You'll want to learn," Mike said. "You can't really understand this place from the surface."

He didn't explain. He turned and walked back toward the framing, and Cole followed, and that was the end of it.

Cole didn't argue. Not out loud. He filed it under things he'd have to face sooner or later.

Later, as it turned out, kept arriving.

The standing seam crew had been on the roof for three days when Cole noticed the gap.

Where two roof planes met at different pitches and pulled apart rather than joining, there was a slot of open sky — six inches wide, maybe eight, running the length of the junction. The foreman had flagged it that morning: cap it with flashing, or leave it?

Cole stood on the scaffolding and looked up through it. A strip of grey November sky. A fir branch at the edge of his field of view.

"Leave it," he said.

"Rain comes straight through."

"Concealed channel along the base. I'll draw it today." He moved along the scaffolding, looking at each junction. "Every one of these — leave them open. But where you're coming over a doorway, solid. No gaps above a door."

The foreman wrote it down.

Cole stayed there a moment longer, looking up through the slot at the moving sky. You'd be standing under the roof — under shelter — and still know exactly where the clouds were. Still feel the scale of the thing above you.

He climbed down and drew the drainage details before lunch.

January arrived without announcement. The sun tracked so low across the south that it barely cleared the tree line — when it appeared at all. Seven hours of flat grey light, the shadows impossibly long even at noon, the crew knocking off early because there simply wasn't enough sky left to work by. Cole stayed. He'd walk the site in the last grey minutes before dark, headlamp in his jacket pocket, checking whatever needed checking.

He hadn't seen the sun in weeks. He stopped counting.

The atmospheric river hit on a Tuesday. Not rain — something else entirely. The gutters overwhelmed within an hour, water sheeting off the roof planes in solid walls. Cole could hear it from inside the construction trailer — a sheer continuous roar on the thin metal walls and roof, the kind of noise that made conversation impossible. He stepped outside once to check the drainage channels and came back soaked to the skin in thirty seconds. The cove had disappeared entirely behind a curtain of grey. The fjord was gone.

He went back to his drawings and recalculated. The downspout sizing was wrong — not badly wrong, but wrong enough. He upsized every run on the east face, added two additional channels along the low valley between the main roof planes, and redrew the drainage map before the rain stopped. The permeable pavers on the service path held. The driveway held. Nothing washed out.

By evening the cove came back, the far shore reappearing first, then the water, then the dock. Cole stood at the trailer window and watched it return.

It snowed overnight in late January. Cole was on site before first light.

The hemlocks had taken the weight the way they always did — branches bowed low, some nearly to the ground, the whole hillside changed into something quieter and heavier than itself. The standing seam roof held the load cleanly, the snow sitting in the valleys between planes. No movement, no creak. The building settling into the landscape the way he'd hoped it would.

He walked the west deck. The snow was unbroken — no footprints, no debris, just a clean white surface over the stone. He stood there a moment, then went to the panel and turned on the heating elements.

He waited.

The snow at the center of the stone began to soften first, then darken, then pull back from the surface in a slow, even retreat. Within twenty minutes, the deck was clear. Cole turned the switch off and stood in the cold, looking at the bare stone surrounded by white.

He made a note in his site binder and kept walking. The hemlocks dripped as the light came up.

They tested the retractable enclosure on a grey morning in March.

Cole had been refining the system design since January — the mechanics, the glass tracking, the sealing sequence for both the walls and the roof panels. It was the most technically ambitious thing on the project, and he'd known from the beginning that drawings weren't enough. You had to see it move.

"Stay on the stone," Cole said. "Away from the edge." Mike stepped back. The control panel was set into the Lodge wall behind them. Cole activated the system.

At the outer deck edge, where the Trex section met the air, the glass wall panels began to rise — silently, in sequence, each one tracking up from its housing without a sound. Then the roof panels followed, moving inward from the perimeter until they met at the center. The seals engaged with a faint click. The wind dropped immediately. Both of them enclosed now — glass on all sides and above, the cove still fully visible, the heated stone warm underfoot.

Mike stood in the sudden quiet. He looked up through the glass roof at the grey sky. Then at Cole.

"Do it again," he said.

Cole retracted the full system and ran it a second time. Mike watched without speaking.

When it was done he stayed on the stone, looking out through the glass. "Still feels like outside," Mike said. "Even now."

"Yes," Cole said.

He was walking back from the site one February night when he saw it — green at the northern horizon, above the clear line of the bluff, the sky beginning to move.

He went inside long enough to get his jacket. Then he texted Mike and Sam: Come over.

They came, Claire with them. Cole's cottage sat on a promontory mid-bluff, water on three sides, the clear ground opening to the north before the tree line began, sky above it all. The lights had strengthened by the time they arrived — green deepening, purple moving in slow curtains, the canal somewhere below them in the dark.

Sam pulled her jacket tighter. Claire stood close beside her. Mike had his hands in his pockets, the way he stood at the end of the dock.

After a while, Sam said, "I've lived here fifteen years and never seen it like this."

Nobody answered. There wasn't anything to add.

They stood there until the lights faded, and then went back inside.

Owen Pierce had been running the Lodge dive shop for years and had the patience of someone who understood that the water would teach everything eventually, if you didn't get in the way.

He started Cole in the pool. Gear assembly, mask clearing, and regulator recovery. The same sequence, again and again, until the hands knew it without the mind. Cole did not enjoy being a beginner. He did not say so. Owen would not have been interested.

"You're thinking too much," Owen said on the third session. "Your body already knows how to breathe. Trust it."

Cole did not trust it. That took longer.

They moved to the cove. Shallow dives first — ten feet, fifteen — the cold a presence even through the drysuit, the visibility murky with tidal sediment. Owen moved through it like it was nothing, which it was, to him. Cole followed and worked on not fighting what couldn't be fought.

"You're not diving," Owen said once, on the surface between descents. "You're learning how not to fight the water."

Cole understood that more than he wanted to admit. He filed it alongside the things that had turned out to apply to more than the situation they came from.

Eventually, the day came when he walked the gravel path from the dive shed with salt drying in his hair and the final certification card warming inside his jacket. He stopped at the construction trailer.

"I'm ready," he said.

Mike didn't ask what he meant. "Sund Rock," he replied. "Tomorrow morning. Early."

They left before the light changed. Sam drove, Mike up front, Cole in the back with his drysuit half-pulled on and the insulated underlayers already trapping whatever warmth he'd started with. The road rattled under them. Gravel popped against the underside of the van.

Mike turned around. "First water shock always wins. The water temperature is only 45 degrees," he said. "Don't fight it. Just breathe through."

"He'll be fine," Sam said.

"I know." Mike faced forward again. "I was talking to myself."

Sam reached back without looking and held out the thermos. "Small sip," she said. "Not a drink."

Cole took it. The rim clicked against his teeth.

They geared up on the shoulder above the entry, the wind off the water cutting through before he got the hood over his ears. By the time he'd cinched the final straps and taken his first breath through the regulator — rubber, cold air, the mineral taste of the apparatus — the sweat on his back had already gone cold. The drysuit sealed him in but didn't keep him warm. It just held the cold at a remove.

He stepped off the shelf and into the water.

The shock was total. Even sealed, the fjord found its way in — not temperature but pressure, a weight settling against every surface of the suit at once. His breath went shallow and fast. His chest expanded, lifting him, and the buoyancy grabbed it, and suddenly he was rising, and his body was telling him to breathe faster, and he knew that was wrong and couldn't stop it.

Mike's fist rose, slow and steady. The signal: ease it down.

Sam had already mirrored it. She hung in the water a few feet away, chest rising and falling in slow, exaggerated rhythm, looking at him, completely unhurried.

Cole forced a long breath in.

Slower out.

Another.

The rising stopped. Mike nodded once. Then pointed down.

They dropped along the line. The surface broke above them into long green fractures, and the sound — his heartbeat, the chop of the water — went away. The cold was still there, but quieter now. Contained.

The kelp rose around them in slow arcs, olive and gold, the fronds moving in long unhurried sweeps. Light came down through the canopy in shifting planes. Shiner perch turned in clusters above the rock, silver-bright against the green.

He kicked forward. A crab moved fast across a ledge ahead of him and vanished under a curtain of kelp. Cole pulled back instinctively; behind her mask, Sam's eyes creased.

A nudibranch clung to a lower ledge — pale, fringed with tendrils that caught and held the light. On the rock shelf beside it, a lingcod lay without moving. Easily three feet. Its jaw was set in a way that suggested patience rather than sleep.

Cole held very still.

The fish ignored him completely.

His breath leveled. His position leveled with it. He stopped working against the water, and the water, for its part, stopped working against him.

Sam tapped her light against a boulder, and a giant Pacific octopus retracted into a crevice, its skin shifting from rust-red to the mottled gray-brown of the surrounding rock in the time it took Cole to understand what he was seeing.

He hovered in the water column and felt, for the first time, something close to weightless.

Then the pressure changed.

Not sharp. Not alarming. Just a displacement — something large moving through the water nearby. He felt it before he understood it. Awareness arriving before the shape.

They came along the Wall in slow certainty: a female, long and unhurried, and a juvenile close at her flank. Their saddle patches caught what light reached that depth, pale against the dark. The juvenile drifted toward them, tilted slightly, and for a moment, one dark eye was level with Cole's face.

He didn't move. He didn't think about not moving. He just held there, looking, while something old and calm moved through him in a wave.

Then they were gone — into the kelp, into the dim, as quietly as they'd arrived.

When they surfaced, Sam pulled her hood back and laughed — completely open, unguarded, the kind of laugh that didn't leave room for anything else in it. Mike broke the water beside them and shook his face clear.

"Does that happen a lot?" Cole said.

"No," Mike said. "It really doesn't." He was still watching the water. "Most people dive their whole lives and never see them underwater. You got that on your first real dive."

Sam was still smiling. She looked at Cole the way she sometimes looked at the cove — with a calm that wasn't indifference but its opposite.

They climbed the steps back to the shoulder. At the top, Sam paused. Out beyond the kelp line, two dorsal fins broke the surface in unison — one tall, one shorter — and rose until the breath came, slow and audible across the flat water. Then they were gone.

"Same pair," Mike said quietly.

Cole stood there, cold finally working through the suit at the collar and the wrists, and felt something settle into place that hadn't been loose before. He wanted to go back under. That was the clearest thought he'd had in months.

Back at the cottage, skin still carrying the chill and the residual sense of green light and depth, Cole unrolled the Lodge plans across the table.

He'd been studying the central bay for weeks — the double-height framing that was already set, the beams directing you toward the water. What he hadn't resolved was what happened above. The ceiling closed it off. The light arrived and stopped.

Underwater, it hadn't stopped. It had narrowed, then widened, then bloomed — a column of brightness rising toward the surface. A lantern shape, if you were close enough to look up through it.

He picked up a pencil.

The void was already there in the structure. He wasn't adding it. He was finding it.

He drew a vertical line from the ridge beam upward, through the roofline, above the building's profile. A tower structure — not decorative. A Light Column, rising above the Lodge, pulling the sky down through its center. He erased a run of interior partitions that had been bothering him since November without knowing why. Every load-bearing point stayed. The bones hadn't changed.

He'd just needed to see them from the right depth.

The next morning , he carried the revised sheet to the construction trailer and unrolled it on the hood of Mike's pickup. Sam was there already, coffee in hand, leaning against the fender.

Mike studied it without speaking.

"The dive," he finally said.

"Yes," Cole said.

"I knew it would." He tapped the lantern tower with one finger. "This is the heart of it, isn't it?"

"Yes," Cole said. "That's what the building is reaching for — that's what it wants to be."

Sam set down her coffee and looked at the drawing for a long moment — the column rising through the Lodge's center, the lantern structure above the roofline, the place where the tower met the standing seam metal.

"There should be an octopus," she said.

Mike looked at her.

"Up here." She pointed to the column, two-thirds of the way up. "Stainless. Large enough to see from the water. Tentacles over the roof." She kept her eyes on the drawing. "This place is named for the cove. The cove is named for them. We saw one at Sund Rock. It should be here."

Cole was already seeing it — the way the steel would catch the light, the tentacles draped across the standing seam, the column rising from its center.

"I know someone," he said. "He owes me a favor."

Mike nodded once. "Then build it. And don't hold back."

Sam picked up her coffee. "The Glass Lodge at Octopus Cove," she said, as though she were reading something already written.

Nobody argued with it. It was just what the place should be called.

He went back the following Saturday. Sam didn't ask why. She just showed up at the dive shed at seven with two thermoses and said, "Wind's low, visibility should be good."

It was. The kelp forest was the same — the slow arcs, the shifting light, the shiner perch turning in their loose formations above the rock. Nothing dramatic happened. A harbor seal came in close and hung there for a moment, regarding him with the mild curiosity of something that lived here and found him mildly interesting. Then it was gone.

They surfaced after forty minutes. Cole sat on the steps and let the cold work through the suit at his collar and wrists and felt, for the second time, that quiet settling — steady and undeniable.

Sam pulled off her gloves. “Better?”

“Yes,” Cole said.

She nodded as though she’d expected nothing else, and they walked back up the hill.

5

OPEN BY MEMORIAL DAY

Sam found Mike at the end of the dock after dinner, hands in his jacket pockets, watching the water go flat in the evening light.

She stood beside him. Neither of them spoke for a moment.

Mike's eyes tracked the kelp line. "Oxygen levels were down again this summer," he said quietly. "Smolt run was thin." He was reading the water the way he always read it — not looking at it but into it. "The fjord's been under pressure for years. Gets a little worse each season."

"He leaves Thursday," she said.

Mike nodded. He'd known.

"End of term," she said. "He'll go back to Seattle and finish out the quarter. And then the question is whether he comes back."

"I know," Mike said.

The cove was still. Somewhere out past the kelp line, something surfaced briefly and was gone.

"He chose the right cottage," Sam said. "Before the foundations were poured. I checked the blueprints from the first site visit. He picked that one from a drawing."

Mike looked at her.

"He knew which one he wanted before he'd ever seen it." A pause. "I thought you should know that."

Sam was quiet for a moment. "He doesn't have people here," she said. Not sadly. Just as a fact she'd been sitting with. "He does now. He just hasn't noticed yet."

Mike was quiet for a moment. "Are you telling me to ask him, or are you telling me you already want me to?"

Sam didn't answer right away. That was answer enough.

"He'll say he has to think about it," Mike said.

"He will."

"And then he'll say yes."

"Yes," Sam said.

The light was almost gone now, the water turning the color of pewter. Above them on the bluff, the Light Column caught the last of the sky.

"Before he goes," Sam said.

Mike nodded once. That was all that needed saying. They stood there a little longer, and then Sam went back up the hill, and Mike stayed where he was, watching the water.

He'd been at another project — a site visit two hours north — and was heading back to the Lodge when he stopped at the marina for coffee. It was a habit by then, the stop, the view across the water while the thermos filled.

The dog was sitting by the entrance. Small, rust-and-tan, with the alert stillness of something that had been waiting specifically for him. Arlo Jensen was nearby with his own coffee, watching.

Cole kept walking. The dog fell into step.

He was distracted, running through problems in his head — the north foundation detail, a question about the mechanical chase — and he made it nearly to his SUV before he noticed. He stopped. Looked down. The dog looked up. Not begging. Just present.

"I have work to do," Cole said.

The dog sat.

Cole got in the Ioniq. Behind him, through the glass, the dog sat in the gravel and watched him go. When Cole pulled out of the lot, he checked the mirror. The dog was still sitting there.

He was at the marina the next morning. And the one after that. He appeared to have no owner and no agenda beyond this specific campaign, and it prosecuted the campaign without urgency, as though time were not a factor.

Eventually, he stopped waiting at the marina. He started waiting at the site instead — at the construction entrance, same posture, same patience. The crew noticed. Cole told himself he hadn't.

Sam left a water bowl by the trailer.

Cole didn't mention it.

One morning, Cole pulled in, and the dog was already there, sitting at the site entrance as though it had been there for hours. It probably had.

Cole walked the site. The dog walked with him.

He didn't get underfoot. When Cole stopped to check a connection, he sat and waited. When he crouched to look at something low it settled beside him in the gravel, close enough that he could smell wet dog and fir bark and the particular outdoor smell of an animal that lived in the weather. When he moved on, the dog moved on. He had learned his pace exactly.

Around midday, Cole went back to the trailer to pull drawings. The dog came and lay down outside the door.

Cole stood in the trailer doorway for a moment, looking at him.

"You're going to be a problem," he said.

The dog's tail moved once against the gravel.

Cole was loading the last of it into his car — the roll of revised drawings, the site binder, the thermos he'd been meaning to return to Sam for two weeks — when Mike came around the corner of the cottage.

He stood with his hands in his pockets, the way he stood at the end of the dock. Not checking on anything. Just there.

"Spring quarter wraps when?" Mike asked.

"Third week of May," Cole said.

Mike nodded. "Lodge opens Memorial Day weekend."

Cole straightened. He looked at Mike.

"Cottage is yours through the summer," Mike said. "If you want it."

Cole didn't answer right away.

"You don't have to decide now," Mike said. "Just wanted you to know it was there."

Cole looked at the cottage — the one he'd chosen from a drawing before he'd seen it, the promontory jutting furthest to the south, water on three sides. The light on the cove in the early morning. The plans spread across the small table at night, student drawings beside them, two lives running in parallel until they'd stopped feeling like two lives.

Cole was quiet for a moment. Then: "Yes. I'd like that."

Mike nodded once, as though that settled something that had been open for a while. "Drive safe."

He turned and walked back toward the Lodge without waiting for anything more. He made the offer and let it sit. He knew when something didn't need tending.

Cole finished loading the car — He had a nine o'clock on Monday. He'd be back on Wednesday.

He stood there a moment in the April cold, the fjord flat and grey below the bluff, the Lodge visible through the firs — nearly done. He thought about Sam leaving food for a dog he didn't have. He thought about Mike making an offer and then walking away before Cole could complicate things. He thought about eight months of someone always knowing where he was on the site without asking.

Two days. He'd be back in two days.

He got in and drove.

Spring quarter wrapped on a Thursday. Cole was back on site by Friday morning.

A week before the opening, Mike asked if Cole wanted to walk the building. Not an inspection. Not a punch list. Just a walk. Cole said yes.

They went room by room without talking much. Mike paused at thresholds, read sightlines, ran a hand along a stone course, the way he'd touch the hull of a boat he was thinking of buying. Cole stayed a half-step back. He'd learned by then that Mike processed things at his own pace and didn't need narration.

They came out onto the main deck. Mike stopped. He looked up.

Above them, where two roof planes met and pulled apart, a narrow strip of sky ran the length of the junction. Clouds moving through it. A branch at the edge of the frame.

"I can see the sky," Mike said.

"Yes."

Mike stayed with it. "From under the roof."

"The drainage channels handle the rain. Nothing comes inside."

Mike looked out at the cove, then back up at the slot. "It feels open," he said. "Even standing here under cover, it feels open."

Cole nodded. He didn't add anything. Mike had just said what it was.

Louis arrived back from Calais five days before the opening. He went straight to the kitchen without stopping at the office.

That afternoon, Cole came through the Lodge and stopped in the kitchen doorway. Louis was at the range, moving between stations with the specific economy of a man who knew exactly where everything was and had already verified it twice. He didn't look up. He didn't speak. The kitchen ran around him in its own precise rhythm. But he was smiling. Not for anyone. Just quietly, over a pan he was reducing. Cole went back out without a word. It was the best review the kitchen would ever get.

Three days before the opening, Mike told the crew to be at the Lodge at seven. Not a request.

When they filed in — Garrett and his concrete finishers, the standing seam crew, the glaziers, the electricians, the finish carpenters — the dining room was set. Proper linen. The good glasses. Louis's full menu, plated the way it would be plated for guests, because Louis did not believe in rehearsing anything at half measure.

Mike stood at the head of the room. He didn't make a speech. He said: "Sit down."

They sat. Louis fed them.

The dog worked the perimeter with practiced patience, collecting what fell. Outside, the cove caught the last of the evening light through the tall windows, the way it would for every guest who came after.

At some point, Cole looked up. Above him, a strip of May sky ran through the gap in the roof planes — still bright, going gold at the edges. The crew that had built it was eating under it.

He looked back at his plate. Louis had outdone himself.

The crane arrived at seven in the morning, the day before the Lodge opened.

Cole had been up since five. He'd walked the west lawn twice, checked the light column housing twice, and was on his third coffee when he heard the low diesel rumble coming up the service road. The dog was already on his feet, ears forward, tracking the sound. Cooper, who had learned to read the dog's posture as a reliable index of how worried to be, lifted his head from Sam's jacket on the deck chair and watched.

Marcus had driven up from Portland two days earlier with Tahoma crated in sections on a rented flatbed — the body in one padded frame, the eight tentacles nested separately like curved pieces of a puzzle only Marcus fully understood. He'd spent those two days in the equipment bay making adjustments Cole hadn't asked about and didn't question. Marcus worked the way Cole worked, and that was why Cole had called him.

The crane lifted the body first. It rose slowly, turning in the morning air — the central mass of her, polished and clean, catching the May light as it swung toward the column. Cole tracked it from the west lawn, hands in his jacket pockets, the dog at his boot, Cooper a half-step behind — the position Cooper always took when the dog hadn't decided to move yet.

The body seated into its housing with a sound Cole felt through the soles of his feet.

Then the tentacles.

Marcus and his crew worked from a scissor lift, bolting each one into place from the body outward — the first two angled toward the roof edge, the remaining six beginning their drape down the column's face. Cole watched each piece go on and checked it against the drawing in his head. The proportions were right. The weight distribution was right. But drawings were drawings, and what he needed to know he couldn't know until the last bolt was tightened.

It took most of the day. The dog slept in the grass at some point. Cooper did not.

Late afternoon, Marcus secured the last tentacle — the longest, the one that would reach furthest over the roof edge — and the crew descended. Marcus backed the lift away and stood on the grass.

Cole looked up.

She was complete. The low western light found all of her at once — moving across the curves and planes of the steel the way it moved across the fjord, catching the tentacles differently as the angle shifted, making her seem to breathe.

His mother's voice came without warning.

Color is how the world lets you know it's alive.

He'd heard it his whole life without fully grasping it. Standing on the west lawn with a dog on his boot and eight months of work finally holding still in the late light, he thought he was beginning to understand.

Mike appeared at his shoulder. He looked up at Tahoma for a long moment. Then at Cole.

"Day before opening," Mike said.

"She's in," Cole said.

Mike studied him with the patience of a man who had survived eight months of construction and learned when to push and when not to. "You cut it awfully close."

"She's in," Cole said again.

Mike looked back at her — the light shifting now, the steel moving through the afternoon in a way that made her seem less like something bolted into place and more like something that had always been there. He nodded once, the particular nod he kept for things that had met a standard he hadn't quite put into words.

"She is," he agreed, and walked back toward the Lodge.

The first guests arrived at two in the afternoon.

Cole was on the Lodge deck when Eldon brought the van up from the Bremerton ferry run — four people, luggage, voices carrying across the parking area in the easy way of people beginning something they'd been looking forward to. Sam was at the entrance, unhurried, doing exactly what she'd been built to do. Irene materialized behind the bar as if she'd never left.

The dog sat beside Cole on the deck, watching. Cooper was already inside — lying near the front desk in the particular way of a dog who considered this his post.

Sam had finished her last exam three days ago. Five years of Resort Management credits accumulated part-time on Tuesday and Wednesday evenings, and then the Lodge closed and she'd switched to full-time — the closure giving her the one thing she'd never had enough of, which was uninterrupted time. The degree and the opening had arrived in the same week. Cole thought that was exactly right for Sam. She didn't finish things one at a time if she could manage it.

He'd waited until that first morning, before the guests arrived, standing at the deck rail with both of them looking out at the fjord.

"Congratulations," he said.

She glanced at him. Then back at the water. "Yes," she said simply. That was enough.

By the second day, the dog had his routine. He walked Cole to breakfast, waited by the dining room door, and followed him to every corner of the grounds. Irene redirected him from the kitchen twice. The second time, she did it without looking up, which the dog apparently took as progress.

Cooper conducted his own rounds — a brief, dignified inspection of each arriving guest, a verdict rendered in the quality of his stillness, then back to his post. The dog watched this procedure with evident interest. Cooper was the Lodge dog. The newcomer appeared to be filing that away.

One afternoon, Sam was on the Lodge deck with her coffee when she saw him. The dog had reached the top of the cove path — the steep one Cooper had never once followed anyone down — and kept going without looking back. Cooper stopped at the edge the way he always did, weight back, ears forward. The dog came back, put his shoulder into Cooper's flank — not hard, just there — then turned and headed down without looking back.

Cooper went.

Sam watched them disappear below the bluff line. She didn't say anything about it. But she refilled her coffee and stayed on the deck a little longer than she'd planned.

6

AND THE LIGHT TOOK HOLD

The Lodge grounds had been full of people all week — guests on the dock, staff on the paths, kids running the west lawn after dinner. The little pocket beagle kept his distance from most of them and stayed in Cole's orbit instead. Cole found this out from Sam, who had apparently been keeping track.

"Forty guests on the grounds," she said at lunch, without looking up from her logbook, "and he's been following you around like you're the only person here."

Cole didn't have anything to say to that.

By the end of the week, the dog had a routine. He was on the cottage porch when Cole came back each evening. He walked Cole to breakfast and waited by the dining room door. He followed him down to the dive shed, up to the point, twice out to the west lawn.

He had a sense for when Cole had been at the drawings too long. He would appear at the screen door, sit, and wait — not impatiently, just with a kind of steady expectation, as if he had consulted a schedule and found Cole overdue for something. Cole always told him he had ten more minutes. The dog always waited him out.

Cole did not feed him. Cole did not name him. He simply accepted the dog's presence the way you accept the weather.

One morning Cole came through the Lodge on his way to breakfast, and Eldon was crossing the lobby in his driver's jacket, keys in hand. He glanced out the window toward the cottage, then back at Cole. "Dog's been on your porch again," he said, and kept walking.

"He does what he wants," Cole said.

Eldon didn't break stride. "Appears so."

Sam watched all of it with the quiet patience of someone who had already reached a conclusion and was waiting for everyone else to catch up. In the second week, she left a bag of dog food in Cole's cottage doorway with a note that said: 'For the dog you don't have.'

Cole put the food out. The dog ate it with dignity.

She arrived on a Tuesday in late June, alone, with a single rolling bag and a canvas tote that clinked with what turned out to be field guides — tide pools, Pacific Northwest birds, coastal geology. She'd booked the east-facing cottage for the full summer. Ten weeks. Sam had noticed because ten weeks was unusual.

She was in her early forties, quiet in the way of someone who had been through something and come out the other side still carrying it. She ate breakfast alone each morning at the corner table by the window, a spiral notebook open beside her plate and a pen moving occasionally across the page. Tide times, maybe. The angle of the light.

In the mornings, she was always at the south-facing table in the dining room — not by request, just by instinct, the way certain plants orient without being told. If that table was taken, she waited for it to become available. When Sam noticed and quietly held it for her, neither of them mentioned it.

In the evenings, she walked the shoreline path past the cove, past the dive shed, sometimes as far as the point. She always came back after the dinner service had wound down, when the grounds were quiet. She nodded to the staff she passed. She didn't start conversations.

One morning, Eldon passed through the dining room on his way to the first shuttle run. Marjorie was at her table, face turned toward the water.

"Good table," he said, without stopping.

"Yes," she said. Then, almost to herself: "The day doesn't seem to mean much without it."

He looked at her for just a moment — the kind of look that takes stock without announcing itself — then nodded and went out.

It was the first time she'd felt like someone had noticed the right thing about her in a very long while.

Sam watched this for two weeks without comment. It was not her business. People came to the Lodge to breathe, and sometimes breathing looked like this: a notebook, a long walk, a corner table, no one asking how you were.

One morning, Sam was crossing the lawn when she saw Marjorie at the water's edge, standing very still, looking out at the cove. Not watching anything in particular. Just standing there with the fjord in front of her and the notebook in her hand.

Sam changed her route slightly. "Good morning," she said, without stopping.

"Good morning," Marjorie said.

Sam slowed. "How long are you with us?"

"Through August," Marjorie said. "Maybe longer."

Sam nodded. Then, easily, without preamble: "We're having a small wedding in July. Just a few people. You'd be welcome."

Marjorie looked at her. Something crossed her face that Sam couldn't quite read — surprise, and something older than surprise.

"I wouldn't want to intrude," she said.

"You wouldn't be," Sam said. "Think about it."

She continued across the lawn. Behind her, just the water and the quiet and whatever Marjorie was carrying that wasn't Sam's to ask about yet.

Two days later, Marjorie stopped at the desk. "The wedding," she said. "I'd like to come, if the offer still stands."

"It does," Sam said. "July twelfth."

Marjorie nodded once and went back out into the morning.

They had flipped a coin. Claire's father walked her first, down the path from the Lodge to the bluff where the lawn opened toward the water. Then Sam and Mike.

Cole stood with Eldon and Irene in the small gathering on the grass — twelve people, maybe fifteen — and watched Mike offer Sam his arm with the matter-of-factness of a man who did not perform occasions but understood them completely. Sam took it. They walked.

She had flowers. Claire had flowers. The dresses were not the same, but they complemented each other the way things do when two people have been paying close attention for a long time.

The officiant kept it short. The vows were their own — Sam's spare and direct, Claire's a little longer, something in them about tides and patience and knowing when to hold still. Cole recognized the language of someone who had spent years watching animals, learning the difference between what a creature needed and what it would accept.

When it was done, Mike shook his head once, slowly, the way a man does when something exceeds what he was prepared for.

Louis had set up a table under the hemlocks with food and something cold to drink. Nobody sat down for very long. People moved and talked, and eventually the afternoon gave way to evening, and the water went gold below the bluff.

Marjorie stood at the edge of it all with her glass, watching. She laughed once at something Irene said — a short, surprised laugh, as though she hadn't expected to. She stayed longer than she'd meant to.

Cole was the last to leave, other than Mike. They stood in the late light without saying anything in particular.

"Good day," Cole said.

"Yes," Mike said. "It was."

Three weeks in, the little pocket beagle found a fishing lure on the cove steps. Cole heard the sound from the cottage porch and was moving before he'd thought about it. Sam had her keys before he reached the Lodge door. Claire got the hook out in twenty minutes. On the drive home, the dog put his head in Cole's lap and went to sleep, bandaged paw resting against Cole's forearm.

That was the night Cole stopped pretending the dog wasn't his.

In the morning, he drove back to Claire's with the window down. The dog rode in the passenger seat — alert, ears streaming back in the wind, bandaged paw extended with a faint air of importance. "Microchip," Cole said when Claire came out. "And whatever else he needs."

An hour later, the dog had a microchip registered to Cole Walker, a record of vaccinations, and a name on the file. Cole had written it without deliberating. It was just the name that fit.

The dog rode home with his chin on the door armrest, watching the trees go past with the quiet satisfaction of a creature who had gotten exactly what he'd set out to get.

Cole had thought, early on, that the dog had chosen him out of need — hunger, shelter, the luck of being near the right person. He understood now that wasn't it. He had arrived with full information. He had simply been waiting for Cole to catch up.

He was back at the Lodge by noon. Sam was crossing the upper path when he pulled in. The dog jumped out first and headed toward the cove stairs.

"Murphy," Cole said — just to stop him, just the name, nothing more.

The dog circled back.

Sam had paused on the path. She looked at the dog, then at Cole. Something settled in her expression — quiet, certain — and then she went on her way without saying anything.

She didn't need to.

Salmonfest had been going on since noon.

By early evening, the west lawn was full — tables down the grass, a band playing above the path, the smell of salmon and wood smoke drifting up from the cooking stations near the beach. Tara Crowley had an oyster table at the south end of the lawn, her crew shucking at a rate that barely kept up with the line. She'd been running the beds off the dock since April, and this was the first time Cole had seen her operating at full tilt — efficient, unhurried, exactly the kind of person you trusted with something that mattered.

Mike caught him looking. "Tara," he said. "Best argument I know for keeping that operation local."

Cole nodded. Filed it away.

The crowd grew as the light softened. Guests from the Lodge mingled with people Cole recognized from supply runs, the dive shop in Hoodsport, and the ferry dock in Bremerton. Murphy moved at his heel, steadier in the crowd than Cole had expected. Cooper stayed close to Sam, and Sam stayed close to Mike, and the three of them moved through the festival the way a family moves — without coordinating, just naturally adjacent.

At seven-thirty, Mike climbed the steps to the small stage above the lawn and tapped the microphone twice.

"Before we lose the light," he said, "we have a winner."

The crowd settled.

"As some of you know, we held a naming contest for our resident octopus." A small ripple of laughter from the direction of the oyster table. "The submissions were reviewed by a very serious panel." He glanced toward the dock where a group of children had claimed the railing. "The panel agreed unanimously. She is — Tahoma."

Murmurs. Then applause. Cole looked up at the column — Tahoma draped across the glass in the evening light — and then east, where the sky above the ridge had gone the particular deep amber that sometimes, on clear August evenings, gave way to something more.

It was there. Faint but unmistakable — the summit in the last horizontal light, white and immense above the dark line of the mountains.

Mother of Waters.

He didn't say it aloud. Neither did anyone else who saw it. Some things don't need commentary.

The band played on. The light continued to fall.

Marjorie was at the far edge of the lawn near the railing that overlooked the cove — her back partly to the crowd, half in the festival and half somewhere else. She had her notebook open, her glass resting on the railing beside her, forgotten. She laughed once at something Irene said passing by, then turned back to the water.

Cole noticed her there. He didn't think anything of it. He filed it away the way he filed things, without knowing yet what he was keeping.

Murphy held steady at Cole's leg. Cooper, who would normally have retreated from the crowd noise by now, sat beside Sam and stayed. Sam glanced down at him, then at Murphy, then back toward the stage with the small private expression of someone watching something she'd predicted.

By eight-thirty, the sky had gone to deep blue, the first stars out, the water below the bluff dark and still. The crowd moved inward without being asked, gathering the way crowds do when they sense something is coming.

Mike came to stand beside Cole. Sam on his other side. Claire just beyond her. Eldon at the edge, hands in his pockets. Murphy on Cole's boot.

The light column fired.

It rose through the Lodge's spine and out through the roof — a clean vertical beam climbing into the August dark, steady and clear, exactly what Cole had spent eight months building toward. The crowd went still. Somewhere in the quiet, a child said 'oh' very softly, and that was exactly right.

The beam held. The fjord caught the edge of it below the bluff —

a faint shimmer on the water, as if the light had made it all the way down.

Cole looked at them — Sam close against Mike's shoulder, Claire with her chin lifted toward the column, Eldon quiet at the edge. Across the lawn, Marjorie stood at the railing with her notebook open and her glass forgotten, watching the light rise.

He didn't have a word for what this was. He only knew he hadn't had it before. And that he hadn't built it. It had simply gathered around him while he was building something else.

None of them knew yet what they would come to mean to each other — what losses lay ahead, what mysteries would unfold, what the fjord would ask of them, what the Lodge itself would one day hold. They were only standing in it together, in the middle of a summer none of them would quite be able to describe afterward.

And the light took hold.

A PREVIEW OF

WHEN SHAPES TAKE HOLD

CLUES IN THE SHALLOWS

Cole stood at the Lodge's deck railing, mug in hand, watching morning light pour across the tideflats below. At the bottom of the ramp, Murphy shouldered into Cooper and the two set off across the sand — Murphy zigzagging with his nose to the ground, ears flopping with each enthusiastic bounce, his white blaze catching the sun as he worked a scent line only he could read. Cooper followed a little further back, twenty pounds of compact muscle with huge paws, his tan coat blending with the sand until he moved, his perpetually worried expression seeming to relax a little.

Cole collected his mug and went inside. Sam was coming out of the service hallway.

"I'm heading out on the Loop Trail," he said. "You want to come?"

Sam glanced up. "Sure. Give me a minute."

By the time Cole reached the bottom of the ramp to the shoreline, boots finding purchase on sand still damp from the tide's retreat, Sam had fallen into step beside him without fuss. The air had that particular northwest clarity that came with high summer — dry and still, everything sharp-edged and present. Salt on the wind, western hemlock warming in the sun, the faint sweetness of madrone bark baking in the heat.

They walked in comfortable silence past the Glass Pavilion — another one of his designs, simpler than the Lodge but sharing its vocabulary of transparency and restraint. Ahead, the hemlock stand rose dark and full against the sky.

"I bet you're glad that's done," Sam said.

"An architect never stops second-guessing, but I think it blends well with the Lodge."

"Those hemlocks are going to save you in the afternoons," Sam said. "That much west-facing glass could cook the place."

"That's why I made sure the Pavilion was built around them."

The West Lawn stretched green and manicured to their right as they started up the gentle switchbacks to the cliffside trail. The path rose gradually, switching back on itself, each turn offering a slightly different angle on the Lodge and the water. Cole had walked this loop dozens of times, but the view never quite repeated itself — different light, different tide, different weather rewriting the scene. He'd designed the Lodge to sit lightly on this land, to frame the fjord rather than dominate it. Some mornings, like this one, he thought he'd gotten it right.

Out on the sand below, Cooper shouldered a bleached driftwood log into place, shoving with his massive paws until it rocked into a better angle. The log was sun-bleached bone-white, stripped of bark, shaped by water into something sculpture-like. Murphy watched from a few feet away, head cocked, clearly calculating.

Then the little beagle sprang, using the log as a springboard to launch up and snag a frayed length of rope tangled in an overhanging branch. For a heartbeat he dangled there, back legs bicycling in empty air, the rope creaking under his weight, until it jerked free.

Murphy looked at Cooper who then planted himself squarely on the rope. Seemingly satisfied, Murphy barked, turned, and ran hard towards the Lodge, then checked himself where the trail crossed his path — nose lifting as a familiar scent pulled him uphill instead. His ears swiveled, torn between two imperatives.

A few turns up, where the trail narrowed and the drop grew steeper to their right, Sam and Cole came upon a woman paused at a narrow overlook. She stood perfectly still, binoculars lifted toward the water, silhouetted against the bright sky.

Red hair escaped from beneath a wide-brimmed sun hat. Everything she wore was practical and clearly chosen with care — lightweight, technical, built for someone who spent serious time outdoors. A dog-eared birding guide rode under one arm, bristling with sticky notes and paper scraps.

Cole gave a casual nod as they passed, the trail too narrow for much more. "Morning."

"Morning," the woman said, lowering the binoculars with a pleased little smile, the kind that suggested she'd just spotted something good.

"They've been busy today," Sam said, more observation than expertise, but friendly.

The woman brightened, turning slightly to include them in her discovery. "Sanderlings on the flats. And a kingfisher — very opinionated."

Sam smiled at that, and they moved past, boots scuffing on packed earth and scattered gravel.

As they rounded the next bend in the trail, where Douglas fir threw deep shadow across the path and the air cooled several degrees, Murphy came pounding up from below. His paws hammered the trail, ears flat, legs churning with the kind of urgency that bypassed all his usual enthusiastic distractibility.

He shot straight for Cole and latched onto his pant leg, yanking once, hard, with surprising strength for such a small dog.

"Okay," Cole said, catching his balance against a tree trunk, feeling the rough bark under his palm. "Okay — what is it?" Murphy released and danced backward, whining, eyes bright and insistent.

The woman's gaze flicked past them toward the flats below, following some line of sight Cole couldn't quite track. She paused, binoculars rising halfway, then lowering again as she searched for the right word.

"That looks..." she said slowly, carefully. "Intentional."

The word landed wrong, changed the temperature of the morning somehow.

Sam's expression changed, the pleasant hiker-greeting mask dropping away. "Where's Cooper?"

* * *

Cole scanned the beach below through gaps in the trees, his architect's eye automatically cataloging distances and angles. Cooper was a dark, planted shape near the waterline, maybe two hundred yards out, not moving like he usually did — no patrol, no investigation, just stillness. "There," Cole said, pointing. "Come on."

They followed Murphy back down toward the Lodge, then turned onto the trail that continued along the waterfront, the air cooling as they dropped toward the flats. The path here ran closer to the water, winding between western hemlock and salal, the undergrowth giving way to beach grass as they approached sea level.

As they passed the Orca Column Conservation Center, its angular cube catching the light, the smell of salt and kelp grew stronger, edged with something metallic. Gulls wheeled overhead, complaining about an opportunity they'd apparently been denied, their cries sharp against the quiet morning.

By the time they reached Cooper, out where the flats stretched quieter and more exposed, the sand firming under their boots with each step, he was planted squarely over the rope Murphy had freed, front paws braced on either side of it. The rope disappeared into a shallow, murky channel where the receding tide still pooled, brown water stained with silt and tannin.

"Oh, you clever boys," Sam breathed. Cooper gave a low huff, as if to say, Finally.

Cole crouched and set his hand on the rope. It was thick and gritty with sand, rough fibers abrading his palm, tension humming through it from whatever weight lay below. The rope was alive in his hand, vibrating slightly with the pull of water and tide.

"Feels like more than driftwood," he said.

Murphy crowded in, tail beating, eyes bright. He mouthed the rope again as if demonstrating, leaving wet marks on the fiber.

"Okay, okay, we see it," Sam said. Her voice had shifted — no longer amused, all business now. "Let's find out what you two discovered."

Together, Cole and Sam hauled on the rope. It rose grudgingly, trailing weeds and bubbles, water streaming off in brown rivulets, until the rusted metal frame of a crab trap broke the surface.

Another trap followed, then another, chained together in a daisy chain that must have run all the way out toward the channel. The metal scraped and clanked as each trap emerged, barnacles crusting the bars, eelgrass tangled in the mesh.

"Someone went to a lot of trouble to hide these under the Lodge's nose," Cole said, watching the chain emerge link by link.

Sam's jaw clenched. "Under all our noses."

The first trap hit the sand with a thud, water draining from its corners. Inside, a tangle of legs and claws scuttled, frantic, shells clicking against metal. Live crabs — their shells still bright, barnacles fresh.

"These should've been pulled weeks ago," Sam said, running her fingers along the frame. "Season's over." She flicked the metal rings with her fingers, the sound sharp and hollow. "And no escape rings. That's illegal gear, full stop."

On top of the crabs, a smaller specimen clung to the bars, abdomen flared, its movements more sluggish than the others. Sam squinted, leaning closer. "That's a female," she said. "They're not supposed to be in here at all."

Murphy whined at the sight of the trapped animals, nails scraping the sand, his whole body tense with distress. Cooper paced a few steps away and back, anxious, his worried forehead even more creased than usual.

"All right," Sam said, more to them than to Cole. "We're on it."

She popped the hatch, the rusty mechanism protesting, and reached in with practiced hands, lifting crabs out one by one, checking size and sex with the efficiency of long experience. The legal ones she carried to the shallows and released, wading in ankle-deep, watching until they vanished into the eelgrass, their shells disappearing into shadow. The undersized and out-of-season she set gently into a bucket of seawater to be turned over to enforcement, counting them as she went.

"Someone set these to kill and forget," she muttered, brushing sand from her hands. "Weeks after closure, down where nobody walks."

"They walk up there," Cole said, glancing toward the trail that climbed the hillside above the flats. From here he could see only the suggestion of movement, people reduced to silhouettes against the treeline, cameras and phones lifted toward the view. "Anybody on that switchback gets a perfect view of the Lodge and this entire stretch of water."

Sam followed his look, eyes narrowing, her expression hardening. "Yeah," she said. "I hate how that suddenly matters."

She wiped her hands on her jeans and pulled out her phone, thumbing it awake. "I'm calling the Sheriff."

"Not WDFW directly?" Cole asked.

"Chain of custody," she said, already scrolling through contacts. "We go through the Sheriff's Office, they dispatch, they call Fish & Wildlife. It keeps things clean."

She stepped a few paces away, enough for the wind to catch her words and tear them into fragments. Cole heard "illegal pots," "live crabs," "below the Glass Lodge," "no, we're not touching anything else."

Murphy watched her, ears tipped forward, as if waiting for orders. Cooper stayed over the remaining traps, shoulders squared, refusing to yield his post, his massive paws planted on either side of the gear like he was guarding evidence.

When Sam returned, tucking her phone back into her pocket, her expression was set. "They're sending a deputy," she said. "Troy Cutler."

"You know him?" Cole asked.

"By reputation," she said, mouth twisting. "Not corrupt. Just likes things simple." She looked down at the traps, at the chain stretching toward deeper water. "This isn't simple."

"What do you want me to do?"

"Stay with the boys." She nodded at Murphy and Cooper. "Don't let anybody come down here and start poking around. I'll keep notes. You — "

She broke off, looking up toward the deck. The Lodge loomed above them, glass walls flashing in the sun, the steel octopus sculpture on Tahoma's column catching light like a beacon, oblivious to what lay below. " — actually, no. I need Mike down here before Cutler gets here," she said. "He's the one they'll really listen to, or blame, or both."

Cole didn't argue. "I'll get him."

* * *

He jogged back up the slope, the incline steeper than it felt walking down, lungs burning by the time the ramp brought him level with the deck. Inside, the air-conditioning was a slap of cool after the exposed beach.

The Great Room buzzed with quiet morning energy — guests clustered at tables, Ilene directing staff from the coffee station, the Eagle Cam playing on the big screen by the fireplace, someone's child pointing excitedly at a fish being delivered to the nest.

Mike stood near the windows, arms crossed, eyes on the water, his profile backlit by the morning sun streaming through the glass.

"Mike," Cole said, catching his breath. "You need to come down to the flats."

Mike didn't turn immediately, still watching something outside. "They get tangled in bull kelp again?" he asked, voice carrying that patient amusement he reserved for the dogs' antics. "You know how they are when it's shedding season."

"It's not kelp," Cole said. "It's traps. A chain of them. Murphy and Cooper pulled up the rope."

That got Mike's attention. He pivoted, the lines around his eyes deepening, the amusement gone. "Illegal?" he asked.

"No escape rings," Cole said. "Crabs still alive. At least one female."

For a moment, all the years showed at once — three decades of fighting for this place, for the water, for the idea that the Lodge was more than a pretty view. Mike's jaw tightened, his shoulders squaring as if bracing for impact.

"Sam's called the Sheriff," Cole added. "They're sending a deputy."

"Of course they are," Mike said softly. He grabbed his radio from the sideboard and clipped it to his belt, the gesture automatic, practiced. "Thirty years, and one bad find below the property line can send us straight down the sewer pipe."

He started for the doors, moving with purpose. "Let's go."

They descended together, Mike setting the pace, the shift from glass-and-cedar to salt-and-sand as abrupt as walking through a doorway in a dream. Down on the flats, Sam stood with her arms folded, the bucket of undersized and out-of-season crabs at her feet, the rest already released. Murphy and Cooper flanked the remaining traps like sentries, Cooper's worried expression somehow appropriate to the situation, Murphy's tail still despite his usual bounce.

* * *

"You took your time," she said to Mike, but the relief in her eyes undercut the words.

"Blame the architect," Mike said, gesturing toward Cole. "We put the deck too high."

Up on the road, gravel crunched. A sheriff's SUV rolled into view and pulled into the small turnout above the trailhead, dust rising from its tires. A few minutes later, a man in a tan uniform made his way down the path, hand resting just shy of the butt of his sidearm, as if gravity simply demanded it. His gait had a swagger to it, boots striking the trail with confidence.

"Deputy Troy Cutler," he said when he reached them, voice easy, chin tipped with the kind of confidence that assumed the world would cooperate. "We got a call about some gear."

Sam gestured to the traps, the chain, the bucket. "Unmarked, no escape rings, still fishing weeks after the season closed. We found live crabs. Females, too." Murphy gave a small huff, as if seconding the complaint.

Cutler squatted and peered inside one of the traps, then eyed the length of the chain stretching toward the channel, his expression unchanged. "Seen worse at the edge of the shipping lanes," he said, straightening. "Folks drop pots and never bother to pull 'em. Could be old junk working itself loose in the tide."

"The crabs aren't old junk," Mike said. He kept his voice level, but anger threaded underneath, taut as the rope had been. "Neither is my shoreline."

Cutler flicked him a quick look, assessing, then reached for his phone to snap a few photos, the shutter sound artificial and intrusive in the open air. "We'll log it," he said, thumbs moving across the screen. "I'll call WDFW Enforcement, let them decide how excited to get. For now, don't move the gear any more than you already have."

"Leaving illegal traps in the water is getting them excited," Sam said tightly.

Cutler shrugged, pocketing his phone. "I'm not saying it's right. Just that it's not the first time someone's been lazy." He tapped notes into his phone, squinting against the sun, then stepped back. "I'll file, they'll read, the machine grinds on."

He nodded to Mike in a way that probably passed for reassuring in his head, then trudged back up the path, radio crackling as he called in his status, his voice fading as he climbed. A moment later his figure vanished over the rise and the sound of his footsteps faded completely, replaced by the lap of water and the cry of gulls.

For the first time since Murphy had yanked the rope, the flats went still. The wind settled. The dogs stopped pacing. Sam exhaled, tension draining from her shoulders as the silence returned, leaving only the three of them and the evidence at their feet.

Whatever came next would not be simple — but the Sheriff's part in it was over.

ALSO BY AVERY WILDE

- When Shapes Take Hold — A Cascadia Mystery (Coming August 2026)
- The Preserve — A Cascadia Mystery (Coming Winter 2026

Thank you for reading *When Shapes Take Hold.*

If you'd like to be notified when the next Cascadia Mystery is available, visit:
cascadia-books.com

www.ingramcontent.com/pod-product-compliance
Lightning Source LLC
LaVergne TN
LVHW041231150826
845673LV00008B/2352